The Cupcake Wedding

Gillian Cross

With illustrations by
Nina de Polonia

Barrington Stoke

For Eli

First published in 2018 in Great Britain by
Barrington Stoke Ltd
18 Walker Street, Edinburgh, EH3 7LP

www.barringtonstoke.co.uk

This 4u2read edition based on *The Cupcake Wedding*
(Barrington Stoke, 2013)

A CIP catalogue record for this book is available
from the British Library upon request

ISBN: 978-1-78112-795-7

Printed in China by Leo

Contents

Chapter 1

Wedding Plans

It was Saturday morning and Holly was baking a chocolate cake. Her sister Mia skipped into the kitchen in her PJs.

"Guess what?" she said. "James has asked me to marry him!"

Holly put the cake in the oven. "What did you say?" she asked.

Mia grinned. "I said YES, of course. We'll get married in the summer!"

"Have you told Mum and Dad?" Holly asked.

"Not yet," Mia said. "James is coming round soon. We'll tell them together."

"You'd better get dressed then," Holly said.

Mia laughed and skipped upstairs. Holly mixed some chocolate icing. 'What will Mum and Dad say?' she thought.

*

"You're only 19," Dad said to Mia and James. "That's very young to get married."

"But they're sensible," Mum said. "And they've both got good jobs. It's lovely news!"

Mum gave Mia a hug. And then she gave James a hug. "Let's have some of Holly's chocolate cake!" she said.

Holly cut everyone a big bit of cake. As they ate it, they talked about the wedding.

"We want to invite all our friends," Mia said. "And all our families too."

"Hang on," Dad said. "Weddings cost a lot of money. How many people is that?"

"Let's make a list," said James.

He and Mia wrote down all their friends' names.

"And there's our mums and dads," Mia said. "And Holly."

"Don't forget Aunty Alice," Mum said. "And your cousins."

James wrote them down. "We *must* invite my football team," he said.

"And my friends from work," Mia said.

By the time they'd eaten their cake, their list had 100 names on.

Dad went pale. "We can't afford it," he said.

"James and I can pay for some of the food," said Mia.

"But there's your dress too," Dad said. "And the hotel and the cars and –"

"Don't worry," Mum told Dad. "I'll make Mia's dress. And we don't need a hotel. We'll have a big tent in the garden."

Holly grinned. "Uncle David can take the photos," she said. "And I'll ask Sally to do the flowers." Sally was the owner of the flower shop where Mia worked.

"My boss will lend us some cars," James said. He worked in a garage. "And I'll ask my mum and Aunty Kate to do the food. They love cooking – except for cakes."

"There's got to be a *cake*!" Holly said. "It's not a proper wedding without a wedding cake."

"We can't have everything," Mia said with a sigh. "We've got to be sensible. We'll do without a cake."

"I could *make* a cake," Holly said.

Mum shook her head. "You're a good cook, Holly," she said, "but wedding cakes are hard to make. We'll need a *huge* cake for all those people. Mia's right. They'll have to do without one."

'No they won't!' Holly thought.

Everyone loved Holly's cakes. Her sponge cakes were light. Her fruit cakes were fruity. And her brownies burst with chocolate. She could make a great wedding cake for Mia and James!

But Holly didn't say anything. 'It can be a surprise,' she thought.

She fetched the rest of the chocolate cake. "Anyone for any more?" she said.

"YES PLEASE!" everyone said.

*

That night, Holly tossed and turned, thinking about the wedding cake. She knew how to make swiss rolls and jam tarts, flapjacks and lemon drizzle cakes. And her cupcakes were the best in the world. But a wedding cake had to be *special*.

After three hours, Holly gave up trying to sleep. She got up and went downstairs.

Mia had left a wedding magazine on the kitchen table. Holly sat down and opened it. The first thing she saw was a picture of a big,

white wedding cake with five layers. It was
covered with fancy icing and hundreds of sugar
flowers.

'HELP!' Holly thought. 'I can't make those!'

Then she turned the page. There was a different kind of wedding cake. It was on a tall stand with ten layers, like a tower. But these layers were full of little pink and white *cupcakes*!

'OK!' Holly thought. 'I can make those!'

But 100 people would be at the wedding. That meant a lot of cupcakes. She might need some help. She took out her phone and messaged Poppy and Tom, her best friends.

Got something to show you. Come to my house before school.

Then Holly went back to bed and fell fast asleep.

Chapter 2

HOW Many Cakes???

Next morning Holly was eating her toast when the bell rang.

"Someone to see you!" Mum shouted.

Holly ran into the hall. Poppy and Tom were at the front door.

"What have you got to show us?" Poppy said.

"Ssh!" Holly said. "It's a secret."

She showed them the cupcake tower in Mia's magazine. "I want to make one of these," she whispered. "For Mia's wedding."

"Mia's *wedding?*" Poppy screeched. "What will she *wear?*"

"Mum's making her dress," Holly said. "And 100 people are coming to the wedding. Will you help me make a SURPRISE cupcake tower?"

"Yes!" Poppy said. "But we'll need a LOT of cupcakes."

"And a stand," Tom said. "Do you think they cost a lot of money?"

"Let's look online," Holly said. "We can do it at school."

*

At lunch time, Holly, Poppy and Tom went to the school library. They found lots of cake

stands for sale on the internet. But they all
cost LOTS of money.

"And they're too small," Poppy said. "They won't hold enough cakes."

"How many will we need?" said Tom. "Let's work it out."

"Well," Holly said, "there's 100 wedding guests ..."

Poppy tried to work it out on her fingers. "How many cupcakes will one person eat?"

"Three?" Holly said.

"More than that." Poppy smiled. "I can eat four."

"I can eat ten!" Tom said.

Holly gasped. "TEN???"

"Easy," Tom said. "People always eat lots of cake. Especially at weddings."

"If we make ten cupcakes per person ..."
Poppy counted on her fingers. "We need ..."

"We need a *huge* stand," Tom said. "Where will we get one that big?"

"I can make one," said a voice.

It was Bella, the school maths whizz. As the others watched, she drew a stand on her computer screen. It was like a very tall tower.

"I'll use old metal trays to make it," she said. "You'll need 25 layers to hold all those cupcakes."

"So how many cupcakes will we need?" Holly said.

Bella looked at them all.

"You'll need a THOUSAND!" she said.

Chapter 3

How Much MONEY???

"A THOUSAND!" Poppy yelled. "How can we make that many cupcakes?"

"You'll have to get everyone in the class to help," Bella said.

"They won't do that," Tom said.

But Holly had a plan. "Let me talk to them all after lunch," she said.

So, after lunch, they ran back to the classroom. Holly waited until everyone was there, then jumped up on the table at the front.

"This is about CAKE!" she shouted.

That shut everyone up!

"What cake?" Joe asked. He loved cake.

"I'm making my sister's wedding cake," Holly said. "And I want you to help me."

"Why should we?" Joe said.

Holly looked round. There were 25 kids in the class.

"I want you all to bake 48 cupcakes," she said. "On the day before the wedding. I'll buy all the ingredients. You'll give me 40 for the wedding and keep the other 8. So you get 8 *free* cupcakes! What do you say?"

"What about the icing?" Joe asked.

"I'll do that," Holly said.

"And I'll decorate the cakes," Poppy said. "I'll make them *really* pretty."

There was a lot of muttering. Then Bella jumped onto the table next to Holly. She had printed out her picture of the cupcake stand and she held it up.

"I'm going to make a tower like this," she shouted. "And it will be four metres tall!"

Everyone gasped.

"Awesome," Joe said. "It'll be the world's tallest wedding cake."

All of a sudden, everyone was excited. They all wanted to help make the wedding cake.

"Fantastic!" Holly said with a grin. "But DON'T tell anyone. It's top secret. OK?"

"OK!" everyone shouted.

Holly jumped off the table – just in time. Two seconds later, Mrs Bennett walked in.

*

So now they had 25 cooks.

'Everything's sorted,' Holly thought.

But Bella was still doing sums..

"You need a lot of stuff for a thousand cupcakes," she said to Holly and her friends. "Look." She held out a list. It said –

8 1/2 kg **margarine**

8 1/2 kg **sugar**

21 kg **icing sugar**

8 1/2 kg **flour**

10 1/2 kg **butter**

168 **eggs**

"Wow!" Poppy gasped. "How much will all that cost?"

Bella looked at her sums. "It will cost £121.80."

"A hundred and twenty-one pounds!!!" Tom said.

Bella nodded. "And 80 pence."

"Where will we get that much money?" Holly said.

"Will your mum and dad give you some?" Tom asked.

"I want it to be a *surprise*," Holly said. "We'll have to raise the money ourselves."

"I know," Poppy said. "There's a big car boot sale on Saturday. My mum will take us. Bring all your old stuff to sell."

*

On Saturday, Holly filled two bags with her old toys. Then she and Tom went to Poppy's house. Bella was there too, with three old calculators and a box of Lego.

Poppy had ten big bags. "They're full of my old clothes," she said.

'Fantastic!' Holly thought. Poppy always had nice posh clothes. 'We'll sell those for lots of money.'

"Wow!" Poppy's mum said when she saw all the bags. "Good job I've got a big car."

The bags filled the boot and most of the back seat. Poppy and her mum sat in front and Holly squeezed into the back. The others waved them off.

"Make a MILLION!" Tom and Bella yelled.

"We don't need a million," Holly yelled back. "Just £121 –"

"And 80 pence," Bella shouted.

Chapter 4

Celebrities – of the
Car Boot Sale

Off they drove to the car boot sale. There were masses of people there already, selling things that looked brand new – games consoles and DVDs and smartphones. Holly's heart sank. Who would buy her old toys with stuff like that around?

Poppy's mum set up their table and Holly and Poppy laid out the toys and the calculators. But they didn't sell anything. People didn't even bother to look. "What rubbish," Holly heard someone say.

'What shall we do?' Holly thought. 'We won't make any money at all.'

"Let's hang these up," Poppy's mum said as she unpacked the clothes. "To show people how good they are."

She tied one end of a bit of string to her car and the other end to a van next to them. Then they pegged Poppy's clothes along the string. They flapped in the wind and people started to look.

"I'll give you £1 for that dress," one woman said.

Holly was about to say yes, but Poppy trod on her foot to stop her.

"It's a posh label," she told the woman. "It costs loads more than that."

The woman frowned. "I'll give you £2," she said.

"£10," Poppy said.

"£5," the woman said.

"£5 and 80 pence," Poppy said. "We're raising money to make Holly's sister a wedding cake."

The woman smiled at Holly. "How sweet!" she said. "I'll give you £6 for the dress. It's so nice of you to sell your lovely clothes to help your sister."

"They're not –" Holly began.

Poppy trod on her foot again. "Sssh!" she said. "I've got an idea."

"What?" Holly said.

"Never mind." Poppy shook her head. "Just stand in front of the clothes – and keep your mouth shut."

Then Poppy asked her mum for a pen and paper. But Holly didn't see what she did with them – because there was a sudden flood of people at their car. Lots of women stopped to look at Poppy's clothes. And they *all* smiled at Holly.

Holly didn't sell anything herself, because Poppy was right behind her. Every time a woman picked out a dress or a top, Poppy said, "£10" or "£5" – and the woman paid what she asked!

In half an hour, they'd sold all the clothes. Poppy counted the money. "We've made a £150!" she said. "We can buy decorations for the cakes too."

"I don't understand," Holly said. "Why did everyone pay so much?"

"Because I'm clever," Poppy said. "Look!"

Holly turned and saw the sign Poppy had stuck on the car. It said –

Please buy these clothes!
I need money for my sister's wedding cake!

"That's so embarrassing!" Holly said. "How *could* you?"

"It worked, didn't it?" Poppy grinned. "Now we –"

She broke off and grabbed Holly's arm.

"Oh no!" she said. "Look who's here!"

Holly saw Mia and James walking towards them.

"Help!" she said. "They mustn't see me!" She grabbed the notice off the car and dived into the back seat. Poppy slammed the door shut.

Just in time! Two seconds later, Mia and James came over.

"Hello, Poppy," Mia said. "Fancy seeing you here!"

"We – er – love car boot sales," Poppy said. "Don't we, Mum?"

Poppy's mum smiled at Mia and James. "I hear you're getting married. That's brave when you're so young."

"We're not *that* young," James said.

"We'll be 20 soon," said Mia.

Holly peeped over the back seat. They were walking off – both of them frowning.

Poppy opened the door to let Holly out.
"That was close!" she said. "If they'd seen my
sign, it would have spoiled the surprise."

"But they didn't," Holly said. "And we've got
lots of money now. We can go shopping!"

Chapter 5

Secret Shoppers

Three days before the wedding, Holly, Poppy and Tom went shopping. They filled their trolley with sugar and flour, eggs and butter and margarine. It was very heavy.

"We've got lots of money left," Tom said. "We can buy really nice decorations."

"Woo-hoo!" Poppy said.

They chose sugar flowers and butterflies and little silver balls. They were choosing colours for the icing when Tom muttered, "*Look out!*"

He shot off, taking the trolley with him.

Holly and Poppy ran after him.

"What are you doing?" Poppy said when they found him at the back of the shop.

"Hiding," Tom whispered. "Mia and James have just come in. They mustn't see what's in our trolley."

"OK," Poppy said. "I'll go and distract them. Pay for the stuff and get out of here – fast!"

Poppy ran off. Holly peered round the corner and saw her crash into the trolley James was pushing.

"Careful!" James said.

"What are you doing?" Mia asked.

"I'm looking for the – um – car polish,"
Poppy said. "Do you know where it is?"

"Of course," James said. He knew everything about cars. "Come on."

As James and Mia showed Poppy the car polish, Tom and Holly ran to the checkout. They paid for all their shopping, but it was far too heavy to carry.

"Push the trolley into the car park!" Tom said. "I'll phone my brother and ask him to pick us up."

When Tom's brother arrived, they put the shopping into his car. Then he and Tom took it home and Holly went to find Poppy.

Poppy was next to the car polish with James and Mia. They were talking to a grumpy old man.

"James and Mia are getting *married*," Poppy was saying. "Isn't that wonderful?"

"Hmmph!" the grumpy man said. "They're too young."

"We're 19," Mia said.

"Much too young!" the grumpy man said. "You'll never cope."

Mia went pale and James put his arm round her. "We'll be fine!" he said. But he didn't sound very happy.

Holly waved at Poppy to show her the danger was over.

Poppy gave James and Mia a big smile. "I don't think my parents like this kind of car polish," she said. "I'll try somewhere else."

She skipped away and met Holly in the car park.

"Let's get cooking!" Holly said.

Chapter 6

The Great Bake-off

Holly, Poppy and Tom took the shopping into school next morning and Holly shared it out.

"You need to bake the cakes on Friday afternoon," she told the class. "That way they'll be fresh for the wedding on Saturday."

"I don't know how to bake cakes," Joe said. "You'll have to show me."

"And me!" lots of other people said.

Holly frowned. "I can't show you all at once!" She didn't know what to do.

But Bella did. "You'll have to make a video," she said. "Then post it on YouTube."

*

So that's what Holly did. On Thursday, her mum and dad went bowling and Mia went out with James. As soon as they'd gone, Bella came round to Holly's house.

"I'll shoot the video," Bella said. "You make the cakes – and explain what you're doing."

It was tricky to talk and cook at the same time. It took Holly AGES to make the cupcakes. She was taking them out of the oven when the front door opened.

"It's Mia!" Bella hissed. "Hide the cakes!"

Holly pushed them back into the oven and slammed the door. A second later, Mia walked into the kitchen.

She sniffed. "What's that?   It smells like cake."

"It's – um – my new perfume," Bella said. "It's called *Yummy*."

Holly laughed – but Mia didn't. She looked upset.

"What's the matter?" Holly asked.

"Nothing," Mia said, too fast. "I'm off to bed." She ran upstairs and slammed her bedroom door.

"Do you think she's OK?" Bella whispered.

Holly didn't answer – because she was opening the oven door. Inside were 12 black lumps.

"Don't film those!" she said. And she threw them in the bin.

*

Bella posted the video on YouTube – and everyone watched it. On Friday afternoon they all started baking.

When the cakes were cooked, Holly and Poppy went to everyone's houses to decorate them. Holly piped pink and white icing on top. Poppy added flowers and butterflies and silver balls.

They looked *beautiful*.

When they got to Bella's house, she opened the door and beamed at them.

"My cakes are ready," she said. "But come and see the stand!"

It was awesome. It was so tall they had to stand on a chair to see the top. It was all painted silver.

"It comes to bits," Bella said. "My mum and I can bring it round in the car. Where do you want it?"

"Mum and Dad are putting up a tent in the back garden," Holly said. "That's where it will go."

"We'll come round when it's dark," Bella said.

"And I'll phone everyone," Poppy said, "to tell them to bring their cakes."

"Good!" Holly said. "I'll go and help Mum and Dad with the tent."

Holly went home – but she didn't help with the tent. Because when she opened the door, Mia was sitting on the stairs. She had her wedding dress on, and she looked fantastic.

Except for one thing.

She was in floods of tears.

Chapter 7

"I Can't Do It!"

"What's the matter?" Holly sat down beside Mia. "Don't cry. It's your wedding tomorrow!"

"No, it's not!" Mia wailed. "I can't do it!"

"Why not?" Holly said. "Have you quarrelled with James?"

"No!" Mia sniffed.

Holly didn't understand. "So don't you love him any more?"

"Of course I love him!" Mia sobbed. "He's the best person in the world!"

"What's the problem then?" Holly asked.

Mia wiped her eyes. "Getting married is a *huge* thing," she said. "Everyone's right. We're too young. We'll never manage."

"Yes you will!" Holly said. "You're both sensible –"

"I don't *feel* sensible," Mia wailed. "I'm going to phone James and call off the wedding."

"No!" Holly yelled. "Don't do that!" Then she thought, 'What will I do with a thousand cupcakes without a wedding?!'

Holly grabbed Mia's arm. "Look – you're nervous, that's all. Give yourself time. Don't do anything for an hour. OK?"

Mia hesitated. "Well, maybe –"

Holly gave her a big hug. "That's sensible!" she said. "Wait here." And she ran off to get her bike.

*

Holly pedalled as fast as she could. She was desperate to reach James before Mia rang him.

46

When she got to his house, she leaned her bike against the wall and was about to knock on the front door when she heard a noise.

It was James. He was sitting under a tree with his head in his hands. Even in the dark, Holly could see he was sad.

"What's the matter?" she said.

James lifted his head. "Oh Holly, I'm so unhappy!"

'Oh no!' Holly thought. "But you're getting married tomorrow!" she said.

"We can't do it." James shook his head. "It's not right."

Holly's heart sank. "Don't you love Mia any more?" she asked.

"Don't be silly!" James said. "Mia's the most beautiful, clever, lovely girl in the world. But we're so *young*. Suppose we can't cope?"

"Don't *you* be silly," Holly said. "Of course you can cope. Why don't you come and talk to Mia?"

"I can't bear to see her cry," James said. "I'm going to call her and tell her it's off." He pulled out his phone – but then *Holly's* phone rang.

It was Poppy. "Hey!" she said. "The cakes are all on the stand. They look fab. Come and see them!"

"I –"

I can't come, Holly was going to say.

But then she had an idea. If James and Mia *saw* each other, they might stop being so silly.

If James came into the tent and Mia was there, then maybe ...

"Get my family into the tent," she whispered to Poppy. "*All* of them."

Poppy didn't understand. "I thought it was a surprise."

"This is more important," Holly said. "Do it – *please!*"

She turned to James. "Don't call Mia yet," she said. "There's something I want to show you."

Chapter 8

Disaster!

James frowned. "What do you want to show me?"

"Something in the tent," Holly said. "You *must* see it before you talk to Mia. But we have to be fast. Can we go in your car?"

James nodded. "OK. I'll put your bike in the boot."

They drove to Holly's house and parked outside.

"I'm not coming in," James said.

"Just to the garden," Holly said. "We'll go in the side gate."

The tent was so big it almost filled the back garden. There were lights inside and Holly could hear her mum and dad talking.

"Come on!" she said to James. And she opened the front of the tent.

In the middle of the tent was the cupcake tower. It was stunning. Its bright silver paint glittered. The pink and white cupcakes looked fresh and pretty. The little silver balls on top gleamed.

"WOW!" James said.

"WOW!" another voice said, at the exact same time.

It was Mia. She was on the other side of the tent, still in her wedding dress. She looked beautiful.

"Oh, *Mia!*" said James.

"Oh, *James!*" said Mia.

They sounded as if their hearts were breaking.

'Oh no!' Holly thought. 'It's not going to work!'

If they spoke to each other, the wedding would be off. Holly started talking – fast!

"Do you know how many cupcakes there are?" she babbled. "A THOUSAND! Everyone in my class made some! We worked it out very carefully –"

"Not carefully enough!" Bella's voice said. And she ran into the tent, shaking her head.

"What's the matter?" Holly asked.

Bella frowned. "When I made the stand, I forgot how heavy the cakes would be. They weigh over 60 kilos! And –"

She didn't have time to finish. There was a loud CREAK! and the cupcake tower tilted forward. Then – SNAP! SNAP!! SNAP!!!

The silver layers started to break off – and cupcakes went *everywhere*.

They flew through the air, onto the floor and the tables. There were silver balls all over the carpet and sugar flowers on the chairs. Blobs of icing hit the sides of the tent.

The biggest blob of all landed on Mia's wedding dress.

"*Disaster!*" Tom shouted.

Poppy screamed. Bella hid her face in her hands. Holly's dad stared at the mess and her mum fainted.

Mia and James looked at the mess. Then they looked at each other.

"We better get to work," James said.

Mia nodded. "Let's get Mum out of the way first."

They took her into the house. Then Mia put on an apron and got a mop and bucket. "I'll start cleaning," she said.

James picked up the bits of the cupcake stand. "I think I can weld this together," he said. He looked round at Holly and her friends. "See how many cakes you can save."

They all worked very hard. Poppy and Holly collected up all the cakes that were still good to eat. Mia and Tom cleaned up the tent. And Bella handed bits of metal to James, so he could weld the stand together.

By midnight, everything looked beautiful again. The tables and chairs and the carpet were spotless. Mia had washed and dried the tablecloths. Poppy put all the good cupcakes back on the stand and filled the empty spaces with flowers so the tower was even more stunning.

"Let's eat the broken cakes," Mia said.

She and James made a big pot of coffee. When Holly's mum and dad came back in, everyone was eating cake and drinking coffee.

"It's all cleared up!" said Mum. "I can't believe it. I didn't know where to start."

"But Mia and James did," said Holly. "They were the only ones who knew how to cope. They're a great team."

James put an arm round Mia. "We can cope with anything," he said. "As long as we're together. Right?"

"Right!" Mia said. And she gave him a huge smile.

Chapter 9

Happy Ever After –
with Cupcakes

So there was a wedding after all.

Mia pinned pink roses over the stain on her dress and it looked even more beautiful. Everyone loved the cupcake tower and there were plenty of cakes to eat. People were full of chicken and salad and chocolate pudding and no one wanted *ten* cupcakes.

When James and Mia had left for their honeymoon, all Holly's friends came round to finish the cakes.

"They're scrummy!" Poppy said.

Holly looked up at the stand. "I'm going to have one of these when I get married," she said. "But it's going to be even bigger."

"Cool!" Bella said. "Can I make it?"

They all looked at her. "Suppose it breaks?" said Poppy.

Bella grinned. "James is going to teach me how to weld. So my next stand will be super strong."

"Fantastic!" Holly said.

She shut her eyes and imagined herself in a beautiful wedding dress, standing beside a tall cupcake tree – with a sugar butterfly on every cake.

All two thousand of them!

GILLIAN CROSS has written lots of brilliantly funny stories about the ups and downs of family life. If you enjoyed The Cupcake Wedding, then you'll love ...

Scream, SCREAM, SCREEEEAM!

That's Mark's house since baby Amber arrived.

And Mark's band has a gig coming up, but everyone is in fighting mood.

Can they find a way to work together on their new song, or will there be red faces all round – not just baby Amber's?

Our books are tested
for children and young people by
children and young people.

Thanks to everyone who consulted on
a manuscript for their time and effort in
helping us to make our books better
for our readers.